Praise for The Imagination Station® books

Imagination Station books are exciting. I like all the action and how Mr. Calvert told people about Jesus.

—Matthew, age 7, Colorado Springs, Colorado

These books will help my kids enjoy history.

—Beth S., third-grade public school teacher

Colorado Springs, Colorado

Our children have been riveted and on the edge of their seats through each and every chapter of The Imagination Station books. The series is well-written, engaging, family-friendly, and has great spiritual truths woven into the stories. Highly recommended!

—Crystal P., *Money Saving Mom*®

These books are a great combination of history and adventure in a clean manner perfect for young children.

—Margie B., *My Springfield Mommy* blog

More praise for The Imagination Station® books

My nine-year-old son has already read [the first two books], one of them twice. He is very eager to read more in the series too. I am planning on reading them out loud to my younger son.

—Abbi C., mother of four, Minnesota

[The Imagination Station books] focus on God much more than the Magic Tree House books do.

—Emilee, age 7, Waynesboro, Pennsylvania

FOCUS ON THE FAMILY PRESENTS

THE IMAGINATION STATION®

Battle for Cannibal Island

BOOK 8

**MARIANNE HERING • WAYNE THOMAS BATSON
CREATIVE DIRECTION BY PAUL McCUSKER
ILLUSTRATED BY DAVID HOHN**

TYNDALE

**FOCUS ON THE FAMILY • ADVENTURES IN ODYSSEY
TYNDALE HOUSE PUBLISHERS, INC. • CAROL STREAM, ILLINOIS**

Battle for Cannibal Island
Copyright © 2012 Focus on the Family.

ISBN: 978-1-58997-674-0

A Focus on the Family book published by Tyndale House Publishers, Inc.,
Carol Stream, Illinois 60188

Focus on the Family and Adventures in Odyssey, and the accompanying
logos and designs, are federally registered trademarks, and The Imagination
Station is a federally registered trademark of Focus on the Family, Colorado
Springs, CO 80995.

TYNDALE and Tyndale's quill logo are registered trademarks of Tyndale House
Publishers, Inc.

Cover design by Michael Heath | Magnus Creative

Cataloging-in-Publication Data for this book is available by contacting the
Library of Congress at http://www.loc.gov/help/contact-general.html.

Printed in the United States of America
4 5 6 7 8 9 / 16 15

For manufacturing information regarding this product, please
call 1-800-323-9400.

Contents

To Joe Terrell,

who walked through fire

—MKH

The Ice-Cream Shop

Beth walked inside Whit's End, a popular ice-cream shop in Odyssey. A long line of Saturday customers stood waiting to order. A dozen other people sat at tables eating ice cream.

Beth looked around for her cousin Patrick. He had said he would be there, but she didn't see him.

Mr. Whittaker waved at her from the counter. Then he pointed to the stairs

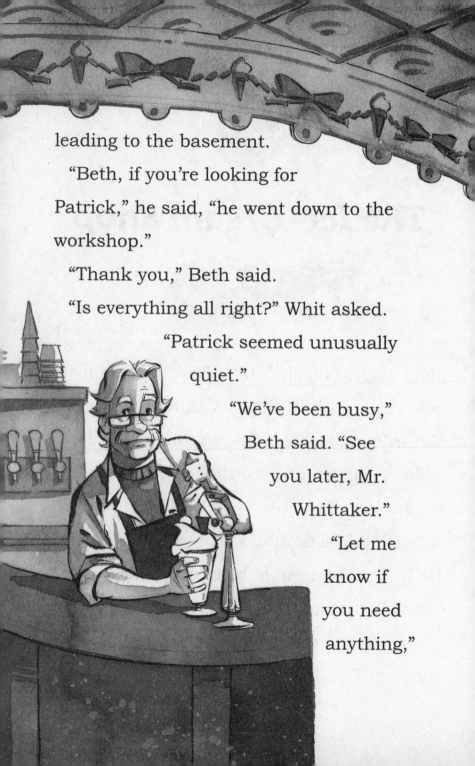

leading to the basement.

"Beth, if you're looking for Patrick," he said, "he went down to the workshop."

"Thank you," Beth said.

"Is everything all right?" Whit asked. "Patrick seemed unusually quiet."

"We've been busy," Beth said. "See you later, Mr. Whittaker."

"Let me know if you need anything,"

Whit said.

Beth walked down the staircase that led to the workshop.

The lights were off.

"Patrick?" she called out. There was no answer.

She flicked the light switch.

Whit's workshop was a large room and took up most of the basement. It was filled with electronic gadgets and parts of broken machines. One of his inventions was called the Imagination Station. It sat in the center of the room.

And so did Patrick. His legs stuck out of the machine's open door.

"I knew I'd find you here," Beth said. She moved closer to the machine.

Patrick was sitting sideways in one of the

seats. His eyes were closed. "Go away," he said. "Can't you see I'm trying to take a nap?"

Beth didn't move. "What's wrong?" she asked.

Patrick sighed. "My mom is making me miss my soccer game tomorrow," he said. "I have to go to a birthday party at Grandma's instead."

"What's wrong with Grandma?" Beth asked. "I like being with her."

"She always lectures me about how I should eat more prunes," Patrick said. "And she says I don't work as hard as she did when she was my age. Plus she pinches my cheeks . . . I have to give up my soccer game for that."

Beth nodded. She sat in the seat next to

Patrick's. "I know how you feel," she said. "I had to miss a sleepover with my best friend because of a school project."

Patrick didn't seem to be listening. "It's an important game," he said. "But my mom said they've had this birthday party planned for a long time." He slumped in his seat.

Beth was quiet. She tried to think of a way to cheer him up. Then she said, "Don't forget I'll be there too. We can sit next to each other."

Patrick snorted. "That won't make it any better," he said. "It'll still be boring."

Beth felt as if the unkind words were a slap in the face. She fought back the urge to get angry or to say something unkind in return.

Patrick didn't seem to know what he'd

said. He reached up and touched a few of the buttons on the dashboard of the Imagination Station.

"What are you doing?" Beth asked.

"Don't worry," Patrick said. He kept touching the buttons. "I think the machine is unplugged."

Beth watched the dashboard for flashing lights. "It's a good thing," she said. "We need to ask Mr. Whittaker before we use this."

"An adventure would be fun," he said softly. "That would take my mind off of how bugged I am."

Beth asked, "Why don't we go get some ice—"

The hum of the Imagination Station interrupted her. The lights on the dashboard blinked.

"What's going on?" Beth asked.

"I don't know," Patrick said. But his eyes lit up. "Maybe the Imagination Station *wants* us to have an adventure."

"It doesn't work that way," Beth said.

Patrick pushed a button, and the doors slid closed.

"Patrick!" Beth cried.

"I want to see what'll happen," Patrick said. "Don't be such a baby."

So now I'm boring and *a baby*, Beth thought.

The lights on the control panel began to flash rapidly.

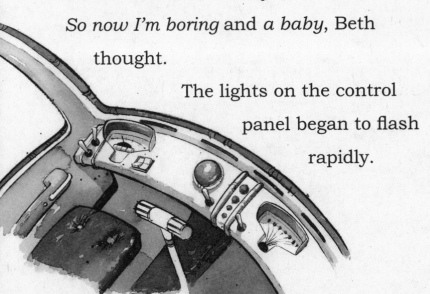

"But we don't know what it's programmed to do," Beth said.

"It probably won't do anything," Patrick said. "Even if I push the—"

"No, Patrick!" Beth shouted.

It was too late. Patrick pushed the red button.

The Imagination Station began to shake. Then it rumbled. It rocked back and forth.

Suddenly everything went black.

The Ship

The rocking motion continued. Patrick looked down. He and Beth were standing on wooden boards. The Imagination Station was gone.

He felt wind on his face and heard a flapping noise. He looked up. Three tall masts held up several square, white sails. Rope ladders and nets crisscrossed the masts like spiderwebs.

The cousins had landed on a large ship.

Patrick looked around. A half-dozen sailors rushed around on the deck. One of them shouted orders to the others. The men had on light-blue shirts and white pants.

Two of the sailors rolled barrels across the deck. A few others were climbing like monkeys up the rope ladders.

Beth yanked Patrick down behind a set of crates. "Stay down," she whispered. "Don't let the sailors see us. They could be pirates."

"Not pirates," he said. "I think it's a British ship. Look at the flag." He pointed to the front of the ship.

Beth looked. A blue flag with a red cross flapped from a short mast. She frowned and said, "It could be a trick. Sometimes pirates flew fake flags to fool other ships."

It was then Patrick noticed Beth's clothes.

She now wore a blue knit cap. Her shirt was made of white linen with the sleeves rolled up. She had on red woolen trousers cut right at the knee. Her feet were bare.

"Look at you," Patrick said.

Beth pointed at him. "You, too," she said.

Patrick looked down. He was dressed the same as Beth. "At least these clothes are comfortable," Patrick said.

"What's this?" Beth asked. A spyglass hung on her belt loop.

Patrick checked his clothes to see if he had anything special. He shoved his hands inside his trouser pockets. From one pocket he pulled out a small object. "Cool," he said. "A pocketknife."

He held it out to Beth. She studied it. "It's kind of old. I think the handle is decorated with some kind of wood."

Patrick opened the blade. The blade was thin. He frowned as he held it up. "That's it? I'd be lucky to pop a balloon with this."

He closed the blade and shoved the knife back inside his pocket. He remembered other adventures in the Imagination Station. He and Beth had been given mysterious gifts.

"Do you think Mr. Whittaker knew we'd take an adventure?" he asked.

Beth shrugged. "How could he know when *I* didn't know?" she asked.

"He seems to know everything," Patrick said.

"Which means there's a reason we're on this ship," Beth said.

Patrick groaned. A "reason" meant learning a "lesson." And he didn't want to learn a lesson today.

Beth peeked around the crate. Patrick crawled next to her and looked around.

"No one's watching us," he said.

"*That* is," she said and pointed. A bright-green bird sat on a mast pole. Its head was cocked. It looked at them with one eye.

Patrick stood up and gazed at the horizon. In the distance he saw an island. It was hilly and green with a gray haze around it.

Beth stood next to him. "Be careful," Beth said. "We don't want the sailors to see us."

"Let's go up, and they won't," Patrick said.

"Up?" Beth asked.

Patrick grabbed a nearby rope ladder. The rope felt dry but not too scratchy. He climbed up to a small wooden platform. The the view of the island was better. It was lush and beautiful.

Beth followed Patrick onto the platform.

"How would you like to take a vacation there?" Patrick asked.

Beth took the spyglass from her belt loop. She put it to her eye. "Something's wrong," she said.

"It looks all right to me," Patrick said.

"I see a lot of people getting into canoes," Beth said. "It looks like they're trying to get off of the island."

"Why?" Patrick asked.

Beth pointed to the right. Patrick saw smoke rising.

"I think the island's on fire," Beth said.

Stowaways

Patrick reached for the spyglass. "Please?" he asked.

Beth handed it to him. "See for yourself. It looks terrible."

Patrick looked through the lens. Colorful birds were flying at crazy angles in the sky. Villagers with dark skin and hair were running away from burning huts.

The men pushed canoes into the water. The canoes were doubled-up and joined together by wood platforms. It had one large triangle-shaped sail.

A sailor rushed to the side of the ship. He shouted, "The cannibals are coming! Get to the ready!"

Patrick gasped and looked at Beth.

"Cannibals?" Beth asked. Her face was pale. "The ones who eat people?"

"I don't think there's any other kind," Patrick said. He looked through the spyglass again. "Big men are on the canoe raft. Some of them are holding huge clubs."

"Are they coming to attack?" Beth asked.

Before Patrick could answer, a sailor shouted up at them. "Hey! Ye lads up there on the foremast."

Patrick looked down.

"Check the spar," the sailor said. "Looks

like it be slippin'."

"Did you hear that?" Beth whispered. "He said 'it be.' Only pirates say things like 'it be.' "

"Shh," Patrick whispered to her.

The sailor below waited for them. He was a young man. His shirt was white. He had a dark blue jacket. His blue hat had a wide brim and a ribbon on the back. A pistol was shoved into the waistband of his white pants.

Patrick noticed that the sailor wore one brown shoe. The other shoe was missing. In its place was a wooden stick that looked like a broom handle.

A peg leg, Patrick thought. *Beth might be right after all. He looks like a pirate. Maybe a shark got his leg.*

"Be quick about it!" the man shouted. "The spar be slipping. Check the rigging!"

"What's a spar?" Beth whispered to Patrick.

Patrick shook his head and shrugged. He called back to the man, "What's a spar?"

"Did me ears hear right?" the man asked. "Ye don't know what a spar be? Who be ye?"

He squinted at Patrick and Beth. He said, "Ye look young . . . and one of ye looks like a girl!"

The sailor thumped his wooden leg on the deck. "Stowaways!" he cried out. "Get down from there. Or I'll see ye thrown into the sea as fish food!"

Patrick and Beth looked at each other. Patrick looked up at the towering mast. He considered climbing farther up to find a way to escape.

"No, Patrick," Beth said, as if she knew what he was thinking. "They might shoot at us! Let's go down."

They climbed down the mast. Rough hands grabbed them.

"Ouch!" Beth cried. "You don't have to pull my arm so hard."

The sailor tugged harder. He began to drag them across the deck. The man's wooden leg pounded loudly on the boards below.

"What are you going to do to us?" Beth asked the man.

"What do you *think* they're going to do?" Patrick asked. "They're pirates. We'll probably walk the plank."

"Pirates!" the man laughed. "Her Majesty's

Navy ran down the last pirate ships
ten years ago. But *stowaways* still be a
problem."

"We're *not* stowaways," Patrick said.

The man stopped and looked them both
in the face. "Ye be on the ship, and ye
don't belong," he said. "That makes ye
stowaways."

Patrick met the man's gaze. The sailor's
eyes were brown. His hair was too, but the
sun had streaked it blond. The man didn't
seem mean, just angry.

The sailor dragged the cousins across the
deck. He nodded toward the large canoe raft
headed their way.

"See that canoe raft?" the man asked.

Patrick looked. The cannibals were rowing
fast. The raft's triangle sail was full of wind.

The ripples around the twin canoes were wide and wavy.

"Yes," Patrick said.

"Those cannibals will keep the captain busy enough. So he'll not be happy to see ye."

"Will he put us to work?" Beth asked.

"Ye may wish for work, but that's not what ye will get," he said. "Naval law says that stowaways must be dropped off on the nearest shore."

"What?" Patrick asked.

"With the *cannibals*?" Beth cried out. "But he can't!"

The sailor shook his head. "The captain be a good man, but he follows the law," he said. "He won't like turnin' ye over to the cannibals. Especially on a holy day."

"What holy day?" Patrick asked.

"*Sunday*, of course," the sailor said.

"Then the captain is a Christian?" Patrick asked.

"Aye," the sailor replied. "Are ye?"

"Yes!" Patrick said. He hoped his answer would make the sailor be nicer to them. "My name is Patrick, and this is my cousin Beth."

"Hi," Beth said nervously.

"And I be surgeon's mate Newland Nettleton," he said. "Glad to know ye. And I'm glad to know ye be Christians too."

"Oh, good," Patrick said, relieved.

Nettleton continued, "If ye be Christians then ye can pray to God for help. Because ye will not get any from the captain—or the cannibals."

The Captain

Surgeon's Mate Nettleton led the cousins
to the end of the ship. Along the way, they
passed a man sitting with his ankles locked
in iron bands. The bands were chained to
the deck.

"Hello, me darlin's," the man said, leering.
The prisoner truly looked like a pirate. He
wore a red-striped shirt and torn pants. He
even had a scarf on his head and blackened
teeth.

Beth sidestepped him.

"Mind yerself, Ambrose," Nettleton said to the man. He pulled Beth and Patrick along.

"As you wish, *Peggy*," the man called out.

Nettleton stopped and scowled. "Don't call me 'Peggy,'" Nettleton said. "Ye know better than to address yer betters with disrespect."

Ambrose laughed as Nettleton tugged Patrick and Beth onward.

"Why is he chained up?" Patrick asked.

"He's a convict. The ship is looking for a new place to put criminals. Today he be waitin' to go to the brig," Nettleton said. "Now, no more talk."

They stopped at a raised deck filled with men. Nettleton stopped at the edge of the crowd.

Beth studied the men in front of her.

Several wore red coats and tall black hats. All of them had rifles.

The red-coated men were gathered around a tall man. Beth guessed he was the captain.

The captain had a round belly and a short white beard. His long hair was pulled back into a ponytail. At least thirty shiny brass buttons were sewn to the front of his blue naval jacket. He wore a white ruffle around his neck. He looked like a cross between Santa Claus and George Washington.

The captain was in an argument with another man. The thin man was dressed in a plain black suit and a white shirt. He didn't look like a sailor or a soldier.

"It's too dangerous, Calvert," the captain said to the man. "The cannibals are killing all the Christians. Not even missionaries are safe. If I put you ashore, you'll die."

"It makes no difference," the missionary called Calvert said. "I died a long time ago."

Beth was curious. Calvert looked tired and terribly thin. But what did he mean about dying a long time ago?

Just then a sailor stepped forward. He took off his hat. "Captain Home," he said, "we've prepared yer landin' boat."

The captain pointed at the canoe raft headed toward the ship. "I don't think we'll be needing it," he said. "The cannibals are coming to us."

Nettleton cleared his throat. A dozen pairs of eyes turned toward him. He removed his blue hat.

Beth pulled off her knit cap. She grabbed Patrick's hat off his head, too. Then she handed it to him.

"By yer leave, Captain Home," Nettleton said. "I just discovered these here stowaways. I brought 'em straight to ye." He pushed the cousins forward.

Beth staggered and then gave a half bow. Patrick stood stiff and stared ahead.

"Stowaways!" the captain said with a boom in his voice. "And one a girl! How can it be?" The captain studied Patrick. "You're not old enough to serve Her Majesty, are you?"

"I'm almost ten," Patrick said.

Captain Home sighed. "You're too young," he said. "Her Majesty's law forbids it."

Just then a blast of thunder echoed across the ocean. Beth looked at the sky. Storm clouds were gathering on the horizon.

"Cannibals, stowaways, and a storm. Can

this day get any worse?" the captain asked. He reached into his jacket. He pulled out a ring with long, thin keys on it.

"Nettleton, I'll decide the stowaways' fates later. First I must deal with the cannibals," the captain said. He handed a ring of keys to Nettleton. "Throw them in the brig with the other prisoner."

"Aye, sir," Nettleton said.

Calvert suddenly stepped forward. He asked, "Captain, surely you don't intend to put this *girl* in the brig with ruffians?"

"I don't have time to play nursemaid," the captain said.

"Then *I* will," Calvert said. "Leave the girl in my care."

The captain thought for a moment, then nodded. He said, "Throw the boy in the brig with the convicts for now—"

"No!" Beth shouted. She linked her arm to Patrick's. "I want to stay with Patrick!"

The captain glared at her. Then he roared, "Child! Do you defy me?"

Calvert suddenly appeared at her side. He crouched down so he was eye-level with her.

"Mind me, child," Calvert said with a warm smile. "Be a good girl. Let Captain Home run his ship the way he thinks best."

He gently pulled Beth's arm away from Patrick's.

Beth couldn't take her eyes from Calvert. There was something about his tone and manner that reminded her of Mr. Whittaker. She wanted to trust him.

Calvert was still crouching. He pivoted toward Patrick. "The faithful man will always find help in times of trouble," Calvert said.

Patrick looked puzzled. "What do you mean?" he asked.

"Remember to say your prayers," Calvert said. "You are never alone."

Nettleton led Patrick away. The missionary put a hand on Beth's shoulder and squeezed it gently.

The Man in Irons

Nettleton led Patrick across the deck toward the middle of the ship. This side of the deck was almost deserted now. The rest of the crew was watching the cannibals.

Nettleton poked Patrick's side with a pistol. "Keep movin'," he said.

Patrick tried to think of a way to escape. But he couldn't. The knife in his pocket wouldn't be any help against a pistol.

"The captain said we're going to the brig,"

Patrick said. "Where's that?"

"Ambrose can tell ye all about it," Nettleton said. "He knows the way well enough."

They moved in closer to the man chained to the deck.

Patrick winced. Ambrose smelled of rotten cabbage. Patrick held his breath.

"I didn't mean no harm before, Peggy," Ambrose said. "Just callin' out one cripple to another. Me leg be a goner. The irons be too tight."

"But not tight enough to keep yer mouth shut," Nettleton said. "Well, soon I won't have to hear yer rude comments."

"Why be that?" Ambrose asked.

Nettleton moved forward. He leaned over and spoke right in Ambrose's face.

"Captain wants ye locked in the belly of

the ship, that be why," Nettleton said with a grin. He shook the keys on the ring Captain Home had given him.

Patrick didn't like the words *belly of the ship.* The brig would be dark. Worse, the other convicts might smell as bad as Ambrose.

"For once I agree with the captain," Ambrose said. "Get me out of these irons. And hurry it up!"

Nettleton had a difficult time kneeling because of his wooden leg. But he crouched low. He could reach the lock on the iron band around Ambrose's ankles.

Nettleton pointed his pistol at the prisoner. "No tricks," he said.

Suddenly a hatch nearby burst open. The head of a large bearded man popped up.

The man looked around.

Nettleton turned toward the sound. Suddenly Ambrose grabbed Nettleton's arm to get the pistol. The two men struggled. The huge man was on deck now and came at them.

Patrick didn't know what to do. "Help!" he called to the huge man.

"I'll help, all right," the large man said. He knocked Patrick aside and leaped on Nettleton.

"Get him pinned, Bryan!" Ambrose called. "Be quick!"

The one called Bryan put his hand over Nettleton's mouth. Nettleton struggled but couldn't call out.

Patrick lay sprawled on the deck. The wind was knocked out of him. He watched

as Bryan wrestled Nettleton onto his back.

Patrick was confused. The one-legged man was gasping for breath. Bryan pinned Nettleton to the deck. The huge man's foot firmly pressed into Nettleton's chest.

Bryan jerked the pistol from Nettleton's hand. "Be still, or breathe yer last," he said.

Patrick stood up. The air came back to his lungs. He thought he should call out for the captain. But the big man aimed the pistol at him.

"Not a word from ye, boy," Bryan said. His face looked like a snarling bulldog.

Patrick snapped his mouth shut. His eyes widened in fear at the pistol.

"Bryan, get the keys!" Ambrose said in a harsh whisper.

Bryan leaned down and snatched the keys

from Nettleton. He gave them to Ambrose.

Nettleton struggled, but Bryan pointed the pistol at him again. Nettleton stopped moving.

Ambrose sorted through the keys. He gave a low growl. "Which one be the right key?" he asked Nettleton.

Nettleton grunted at him.

"Be quick, Ambrose," Bryan said. "Our luck might run out, and Captain Home will send us to a deserted island."

"This be the one!" Ambrose said and shoved the key into the lock. He was free in an instant. He scowled and asked, "Now, what shall we do with Peggy and this boy?"

The Cannibal King

On the other side of the ship, Captain Home and the crew had turned their attention to the cannibals. The canoe was near the ship now.

Calvert kept his hand on Beth's shoulder. He seemed to sense that she might run off if he let go.

"You can see better through the firing hole next to that cannon," he said to her. "It's not often one gets to see cannibals."

Beth paused for a moment. *It's true*, she thought. *Patrick would have stayed to see this if he could.*

She moved over to a long black cannon. She scooted close to its firing hole. Then she poked her spyglass through to watch the approaching canoes.

The canoes were filled with baskets and barrels. Beth also saw a couple of log drums. Most of the men were sitting and rowing. Only three men were standing.

The man in the middle had the tallest, frizziest hair. He had the biggest necklace too. Beth thought the man must be their leader.

The cannibal grinned and showed his white teeth. A shiver of fear went up Beth's neck.

Captain Home and Calvert waited
by the ship's railing.

When the canoes got close, Beth stood up.
She moved near the railing to watch and
listen.

The leader of the canoe raft called out in a
strange language.

Captain Home turned to Calvert. "Will
you translate for me?" he asked.

Calvert nodded. "The chief is called Toki,"
he said. "He brings you a great tribute. He
offers you the finest food and turtle shells
his tribe has to offer."

The captain grunted. "What does Toki
want in return?" he asked.

"To come aboard the ship. He wants
to talk to you as one leader to another,"

Calvert said. "He also wants to send a message to Queen Victoria."

"What message?" Captain Home asked.

Calvert called out to Toki in the strange language. Beth wondered how he knew it.

Toki answered. Calvert listened, and then he translated. "He wants Queen Victoria to give him five thousand rifles."

Five thousand rifles? Beth wondered. *How many people does this chief want to kill?*

Captain Home laughed. "Toki burned down a Christian village on his own island," he said. "Does he really expect Her Majesty to give him weapons?"

"Toki thinks of himself as a great king," Calvert said. "How will you answer him?"

The captain's face flushed red with anger. "A king?" he said. "King of the devils maybe.

He's a disgrace to the human race."

Captain Home slammed a fist on the deck railing. "He's the last cannibal king under Queen Victoria's rule," he said. "He will never come aboard my ship and defile it."

Calvert turned to Toki. Then Calvert paused and looked at the captain again. "Before I give your message, I will ask you once again. May I go with Toki back to his island on Fiji? I want to minister to the Christian Fijians whose huts have burned."

Captain Home frowned at Calvert. "I've already told you no," he said in a stern voice. "I will not leave you on an island full of cannibals. Tomorrow I'll return you to your village, to be with your family."

"So be it," Calvert said with a sigh. He turned to Toki and then a strange thing happened. Calvert didn't speak in the native language. Instead he called out in English.

"Toki," Calvert said, "the captain asks you to stop your war. And so do I. But the one true God asks you to stop killing. He asks that you love your enemies."

Toki answered in English. "I do not care what you or your captain or your God want," he said. "Burning down the Christian village gave me great pleasure."

"The heathen speaks English?" Captain Home shouted at Calvert.

The cannibal king waved a large black club at Calvert. "I hate the Christian people," he shouted back. "I hate your God."

Beth gasped. She had never heard anyone say he hated God. Thunder rolled above them. Beth wondered if God might strike

Toki dead with a lightning bolt.

Calvert leaned heavily on the rail. "Beware, my friend," he said to Toki. "The one true God will not be mocked."

At that moment, thunder crashed. Beth jumped, startled. She looked up at the storm clouds. They were tall and dark and moving toward the island. She wondered if the storm was a typhoon.

King Toki sat down on a canoe bench. His men paddled to turn the canoe raft around.

"I hope that's the last I ever see of him," Captain Home said to Calvert.

Calvert sighed. "I hope to see him every day in heaven," Calvert said. "God loves the cannibals, Captain. Even if you don't."

The captain eyed Calvert. The captain said, "You are a strange and difficult man."

Overboard

Bryan waved the pistol at Patrick and Nettleton. "Both of ye! Move it!" Bryan shouted. "Ye get to be our hostages in case we be caught."

Ambrose was standing now, but his legs looked wobbly. "Get goin', Peggy," he said.

Patrick offered Nettleton his hand. Nettleton grabbed it and pulled. At the same time, he pushed himself up with his good leg.

"Thank ye, lad," Nettleton whispered to Patrick. "Sorry for bunglin' me job. I'll see us out of this mess. Trust me."

"Shut yer fish face," Ambrose said. "Bryan and me, we'll do the talkin'."

Bryan and Ambrose led Patrick and Nettleton to the side of the ship. A landing boat hung about twenty feet over the water. It was attached to the ship with rope and pulleys.

This must be the landing boat that the captain didn't need, Patrick thought.

"Be quick," Bryan said to Ambrose. "The captain won't be talkin' to the cannibal king much longer."

"By the stars, this be our lucky day," Ambrose said.

Bryan poked Patrick's ribs with the pistol.

"Get to the boat," Bryan said. "Move it."

A small platform jutted out from the side of the ship. Patrick climbed over the railing to reach the platform. Then he took a giant step.

He stepped into the boat, and it quickly tilted. Patrick grabbed the side of the boat. Then he sat down to keep his balance.

Patrick watched from the boat as Nettleton, Bryan, and Ambrose climbed onto the small platform.

"Ye be next," Ambrose told Nettleton.

Nettleton stretched his good leg into the boat. Just then a blast of thunder shook the air.

Ambrose and Bryan looked up at the approaching storm clouds.

Nettleton took that moment to act. He

grabbed a boat paddle and hit Bryan full force. Bryan dropped to his knees. The pistol fell from his hand.

Nettleton swung the paddle again. He hit Ambrose in the gut. Ambrose doubled over, gasping for breath.

Nettleton turned around. "Quick, Patrick!" he shouted. "Help me!"

As Patrick stood up, Bryan shoved Nettleton. Nettleton fell into the boat.

The boat swung wildly. Patrick lost his balance. He stumbled backward. The boat tipped over. Suddenly Patrick was falling.

Patrick closed his eyes. He hit the water. *Splash!*

The Storm

Beth watched the cannibals row away from the ship. The muscular men paddled the oars quickly. She wished Patrick could have seen Toki.

On the deck, Captain Home clapped his hands. Beth turned her eyes toward the captain.

"All right, men," Captain Home said. "Time to batten down the hatches. We have a storm blowing in."

The sailors scrambled across the deck and up the rigging. Some rolled up the sails and tightened ropes. Others closed the hatches.

Only Beth, Captain Home, and Calvert remained on the upper deck. Beth turned to the missionary and asked, "Mr. Calvert, why did you want to go with the cannibals? They seem so dangerous."

Calvert looked down at Beth and patted her head. "The cannibals are a dangerous tribe," he said. "But I am a missionary. I must preach the gospel to them. I've shown them God's love by teaching them the Bible and English. I have done so for twelve years. And so far, God has protected me."

"What did you mean when you said you had already died?" Beth asked.

Calvert smiled. "What I meant was that

I'm a Christian," he said.

"So am I," Beth said. "But I'm not dead."

Calvert chuckled. "If you're Christian, then you are quite dead," he said.

Beth crinkled her nose in confusion. "What do you mean?" she asked.

"When I became a Christian," Calvert said, "I gave up my life. My old life of selfishness died. But now, I'm alive in Christ. I live for Him."

"Even if the cannibals kill you?" Beth asked.

Calvert nodded.

"So if you die, you live for Jesus," Beth said. "And if you die while living, that's okay?"

Calvert laughed. "That's right," he said.

His laughter ended when a thunderclap

shook the ship.

Beth looked up at the sky. The storm clouds were dark and angry. She shivered.

Captain Home came over to them. "The two of you must get below deck," he said. "This storm will rock the ship."

"Is Patrick going to be all right?" Beth asked.

"The brig is at the center of the ship," Captain Home said. "The prisoners will be safe enough."

Then the captain gave a small snort. "Where is Nettleton?" Captain Home asked. "It's not like him to dally. I want my keys."

Just then a red-coated soldier jumped onto the deck from the rigging. He rushed over to Captain Home.

The soldier was holding a blue hat in his

hand. He was out of breath. He took off his own black hat. The sergeant had red hair and big ears. His uniform was perfectly neat and clean.

"Sergeant Dunn reporting, sir," the soldier said with a salute. "We've captured two convicts attempting to escape."

Captain Home frowned and said. "Who?"

"Ambrose and Bryan," Dunn said.

"Nettleton had charge of Ambrose," Captain Home said. "Where is he?"

Sergeant Dunn held up the blue hat as if it explained everything. He said, "Nettleton and the stowaway fell overboard in the struggle."

Beth gasped. *Overboard!* she thought.

Patrick struggled to breathe. One minute

he was in the water. The next minute he was grabbed and thrown onto something hard. He was on his back. Black spots grew large in front of his eyes. He saw a face. Then the iron gray sky.

"Breathe! Breathe!" he heard someone shout. Whoever it was kept pushing on his stomach.

Patrick's stomach lurched. He turned his head. Up came a stream of saltwater. It gushed all over the wooden planks.

Patrick gasped for air. He wheezed and fought to breathe in and then out again. His head pounded. His eyes stung.

"Ye must have said yer prayers," Nettleton said.

Patrick felt sick. He blinked his eyes to clear away the salty sting. Then he looked around his surroundings.

He and Nettleton were on the curved bottom of the landing boat. It had somehow flipped over. They were floating on the ocean between the ship and the island. Both were a good distance away.

"What happened?" Patrick asked.

"I pushed the water out of ye," Nettleton said. "That let the air in."

Patrick carefully sat up. "I'm a prisoner, and you still saved me?" he asked.

"Don't let me peg leg fool ye," Nettleton said. "I be an able swimmer. I can't say the same for Bryan and Ambrose."

Patrick was alarmed. "Did they drown?" he asked.

"No. They still be on the ship," Nettleton said. "They can't swim without a barrel tied to 'em," Nettleton said.

Patrick looked out at the ocean. The wind was blowing harder, and the waves rose higher.

"What are we going to do now?" Patrick asked. "How do we get back to the ship?"

"The oars be gone," Nettleton said. "We can't row back.

Suddenly, a huge wave lifted the boat.

Shark!

Captain Home scratched his white beard. He was looking through a spyglass toward the island. "There they are," he said. "Their boat is overturned. They're on top."

"Or the bottom, as the case may be," Calvert said.

Beth unhooked the spyglass on her belt. She searched in the area where the captain had been looking.

She saw Patrick and Nettleton. They were

scrambling to stay on top of the overturned boat.

The captain looked through the spyglass again. "I can't send out a rescue party in time to save them from the storm," the captain said. "We'll have to hope they make it to the island."

"That's all? We have to do *something*!" Beth cried.

Calvert stepped forward. "Captain," he said, "even if they survive the storm, you can't leave them on the cannibals' island alone. May I suggest that we gather a group of soldiers? We can take a rescue boat. Surely they are hardy fellows and can row fast enough to outrun the storm."

Captain Home thought for a moment. "It's still dangerous."

"Nettleton is one of your best men," Calvert said. "You can't leave him at the mercy of the cannibals."

"The same with my cousin," Beth said.

"I'll go with the soldiers," Calvert said, "I can ask the good Fijians for help."

"You're determined to land on that island no matter what happens," the captain said.

"All in the line of duty," Calvert said.

The captain frowned. Then he nodded. "You had better hurry, then. The storm won't wait for you."

The men marched off. They seemed to forget about Beth. She slipped back behind the cannon to stay out of view.

Whatever it takes, she thought, *I'm getting on that rescue boat.*

Then she remembered Patrick and the

wave. She said a quick prayer for his safety. Then she turned to the water and lifted the spyglass to her eye.

Patrick felt the water close over his head again. He thrashed his arms, trying to get to the surface. He broke through and gasped for air.

"Get out of the water," Nettleton shouted. "Before ye get yer leg bit off! There be sharks in these waters!"

Just then, a fin surfaced. Patrick could see a dark form in the water. *Shark!* he thought and trembled.

"I'm trying," Patrick gasped. He swallowed a mouth of saltwater instead.

Patrick frantically dog-paddled as he reached for the rim of the boat.

Nettleton grabbed him by the collar and pulled him onto the boat.

Patrick found a safe spot. He looked over the side of the boat. "That's a big shark!" he said. "It's like a whale!"

Nettleton chuckled. "Aye, that be a whale shark, mate. It made the wave," he said. "They'll knock yer boat around, but they won't eat ye."

Patrick pointed at Nettleton's peg leg. "Is that how you lost your leg?"

"Ye mean from a shark?" Nettleton asked.

Patrick nodded.

"No, me story be not so grand," Nettleton said.

"I had an accident

aboard the ship some years ago. Me leg was crushed. A good surgeon did the honors of cuttin' it off." Nettleton made a slicing motion with his hand. "That saved me dyin' of infection. So now I be learnin' to be a surgeon meself. I want to be helpin' others."

"Isn't it hard?" Patrick asked. "Working on a ship with only one leg? Didn't you want to go home?"

"Home? The ship be me home," Nettleton said. "And the captain had reason to pack me off to England. But he kept a place for me. Even with me bein' a poor cripple. Not everyone be so kind."

Patrick looked toward the ship. It seemed even farther away. "Will the captain rescue us?" he asked.

"He'll do his best," Nettleton said. "But this

storm be a bad one. He might not send a rescue party until dawn."

Patrick frowned. "Then what are we going to do?"

Nettleton glanced to the island. It was getting closer. "Spend the night on that island, I reckon," he said.

"Near *cannibals*?" Patrick asked.

"Do ye have a better plan?" Nettleton asked.

"No," Patrick said. He frowned. "I don't."

The Canoes

There was a moment—just one—when no one was near the rescue boat. Beth crept quickly across the landing. She jumped into the boat. It swayed under her feet. She steadied herself.

The rescue boat had been packed with a few barrels, some tarps, and a trunk.

Where should I hide? Beth wondered. She saw a bench at the back. It was like a shelf. She crawled over to it and then under. She saw the trunk. She pulled it closer to help hide her.

Beth heard footsteps. The soldiers and sailors scrambled into the rescue boat. She could see only their legs as they took position.

She recognized Calvert's black pants and shoes. He sat on the bench above her.

The boat suddenly jerked. Then it jerked again and again. Beth realized the boat was being lowered to the water. There was a small splash, and the boat rocked for a moment.

Beth saw the men's hands reach down to pick up oars. She heard the oars splash in a steady rhythm.

After a few minutes, the rain started. It came in sprinkles first. Then it poured down by bucketfuls. A giant puddle grew around

Beth. It was full of dirt, wood chips, and something green. *Yuck!* she thought.

Lightning flashed somewhere nearby. Thunder rolled. The boat rocked wildly. The trunk looked as if it might tip over. She reached out to steady it.

Suddenly Calvert's feet turned at an angle. Then his face appeared in front of her. Calvert was looking at her upside down.

"Well, well," he said.

Patrick and Nettleton were almost to the island when it began to rain hard. Lightning flashed again and again. After each bolt, thunder boomed. The wind howled. Large waves rocked the boat.

Nettleton jumped off the back of the boat. The water came up only to his knees.

Patrick leaped into the water too. He and Nettleton struggled toward the beach. Waves crashed all around them.

Patrick collapsed on the wet sand. He turned in time to see a large wave grab the boat. It hurled the boat onto a jagged reef. The boat broke apart with a hollow *crack*.

The rain felt like needles stabbing Patrick's skin. Gusts of wind pushed him forward as he collapsed onto shore.

Nettleton walked slowly. His peg leg sunk into the wet sand with each step.

Patrick was soaked through and through. He shivered.

Patrick wished he hadn't pushed the red button on the Imagination Station. He had wanted an adventure, but not one like this.

71

"Would you like a tarp?" Calvert asked Beth. "You'll stay drier."

Beth blushed. She climbed out from her hiding place. Her hair and clothes were sopping wet. She plopped down on the wood bench next to Calvert.

The missionary had a white tarp draped across his head and shoulders.

"How did you know I was there?" Beth asked.

Calvert gave her a wink. "I saw you reach for the trunk," he said. He handed a tarp to Beth.

"Are you going to take me back to the ship?" Beth asked.

"I couldn't even if I wanted to," Calvert said. "We've come too far."

Beth wrapped herself up in the tarp

tent-style. She left a small opening in the front so she could see. The sailors craned their necks to look back at her. One or two scowled.

"I had to come," Beth said. "Patrick is on the island."

Calvert nodded. "God seems determined to keep you in my care," Calvert said. "And I think you're safe enough. God has this little boat in the palm of His hand. He can calm the sea should He choose to do so."

The sailors began to sing a song about a mermaid. The men rowed in time to the music.

Beth tried to forget she was very cold and wet. She thought about Patrick and hoped he was safe.

"Do you think Patrick and Nettleton are all

right?" Beth asked Calvert.

"If the Lord wills it," Calvert said.

Beth took out her spyglass. She searched the water and the shore for signs of Patrick. But seeing anything was difficult because of the rain.

She saw waves with white caps. She saw trees bent by the wind. She saw a dolphin jump out and back into the sea.

No, not a dolphin, she thought. It was one of the cannibals' canoe rafts! It tossed about in the waves.

"I see Toki's canoe," Beth shouted to Calvert. "It's empty!"

Beth handed the spyglass to the missionary. She pointed in the direction he should look.

Calvert peered through the spyglass. Then

he lowered it and looked at Beth. "I'm afraid the sea has swallowed Toki and his men," he said.

The rain fell harder. Patrick followed Nettleton into the palm trees lining the beach. The trees didn't give Patrick much cover from the rain. He looked around. Tangled branches had been ripped from their tree trunks. The wind had torn one palm tree out of the ground.

"We must find shelter!" Nettleton shouted.

Patrick imagined what might happen if they found shelter near the cannibal village. "Where do the cannibals live?" he asked.

"Where do cannibals live?" Nettleton shouted with a laugh. "Wherever they want to!"

A gust of wind pushed Nettleton against a tree trunk. "If ye be a prayin' lad, now be a good time to do it."

Patrick remembered Calvert's words. He said Patrick would never be alone if he prayed. So he did.

Then another gust of wind nearly knocked him down.

"This way!" Nettleton cried.

Patrick turned. His eye caught something moving on the beach. Parts of the cannibals' giant canoe raft washed up on the shore.

"Look!" Patrick shouted at Nettleton.

"What ye be waitin' for?" Nettleton shouted. "Grab 'em!"

Patrick ran to the beach. He tugged at the smallest canoe, but it was heavy. Nettleton joined him. Together they dragged two canoes up the beach.

"We'll turn 'em around so the hollow parts be away from the wind!" Nettleton shouted. "Then we'll wedge 'em between the trees.

"There are baskets tied down inside," Patrick said.

"We'll open 'em in the mornin'," Nettleton said. "Now, help me."

They worked hard and got the job done.

The canoes were now mini-shelters.

Nettleton crawled into one canoe.

Patrick climbed into the other. He had to share the space with the baskets tied down with heavy rope. He didn't mind. He was protected from most of the wind and rain.

Patrick remembered to thank God for bringing them this far safely. Then he fell asleep.

The Cave

Beth didn't know how long it took them to get to the island. But it was dusk when they landed. She was thankful the rescue boat got there safely.

In the darkness of the storm, she had lost all sight of Patrick and Nettleton. The sailors on the rescue boat had to guess where they might have landed.

Beth hopped out of the boat. The wind and the waves knocked her around. Calvert took her arm to hold her steady. They clutched the tarp around them.

She thought she heard the sound of drums. *No,* Beth thought, *that must be thunder.*

She reached the beach. She bent low to look for Patrick's footprints in the sand. But the wind and rain had smoothed away any signs of life.

The sailors unloaded the cargo from the boat. Calvert pulled away from Beth. He left the tarp hanging from her shoulders.

He went to the men and called out, "This way! I know where there's a cave!"

Calvert led the way through the trees. The soldiers and sailors carried the barrels and trunk.

Beth looked around for Patrick. Sergeant

Dunn and three other soldiers held up their rifles. Beth wondered if they expected to be attacked. She also wondered if the rifles would fire in all of this rain.

They came to the bottom of a hill. Tucked inside a tangle of branches and vines was a cave. The soldiers went in first to make sure it was safe. Then they signaled for everyone else to enter.

The cave was dark and moist. It smelled moldy.

One of the sailors quickly opened the barrel lids. Inside them were dried meat, gunpowder, and water.

There was already a ring of stones on the floor of the cave. Two sailors used it to build a fire. They found dried tree branches scattered on one side of the cave.

Calvert and the men gathered at the back of the cave. Beth heard them talking about how to find Nettleton and Patrick. But no one was going out to look now. They would have to wait until morning.

Beth stood near the fire and warmed herself. She studied the cave by firelight. The rock walls were milk-colored with brown streaks. It reminded her of maple syrup.

Suddenly the cave was filled with shouts.

"Woi! Woi! Woi!"

"Bole! Bole!"

Beth spun around toward the mouth of the cave.

Six Fijians with big hair and bigger spears stood in the opening.

"Yi! Yi! Yi!" one of them shouted. Then he rushed in.

Beth screamed.

The Fijians yelled in return. The cave echoed with shouts and whoops.

Suddenly a shot was fired. *Bam!*

The Fijians froze as the sound exploded from wall to wall.

Beth clapped her hands over her ears. She dropped to the ground. She covered her head with her arms.

"Stop in the name of Her Majesty, Queen Victoria," Sergeant Dunn shouted. "I command you to drop your spears!"

Beth lifted her face from the dirt to watch.

The Fijians dropped their spears. Then they each dropped to one knee.

"Don't shoot!" a Fijian man said in English. "We are Christians!"

Calvert worked his way to the cave

entrance. "Don't hurt them," he said to the soldiers. "These men were my English students. And my friends."

"Friends?" Dunn asked. "Why do they have spears? Why were they shouting?"

"Fijians are noisy people," Calvert said. "They are just happy. As am I. And they have spears to defend themselves. They need protection from wild animals and Toki and his men."

Calvert motioned for the Fijians to stand.

They stood up and left their spears at their feet. Calvert embraced the men one by one.

Beth stood up and moved closer to Sergeant Dunn. Calvert might be mistaken about the Fijians. If he was, she wanted to be close to the men with the rifles.

Calvert spoke to the Fijians in their own

language. They gestured with their hands. They all seemed to talk at once.

Then there was silence. Beth realized they were looking at her. Their dark eyes were full of concern.

Calvert gazed at her too.

"What?" Beth asked. "Why is everyone looking at me?"

Calvert said, "The Fijian drums have given them news about Toki."

"You mean they really send messages with drums?" Beth asked.

Calvert nodded, then said, "Toki is alive."

"Then why was everyone looking at me?" Beth asked.

"Toki is hunting for Patrick and Nettleton," Calvert said.

A Prisoner

Patrick woke when Nettleton gently shook him. "Get up," Nettleton said. "I need yer help to make a fire. That way the ship's watchmen will spot us."

Patrick sat up straight. *Thud!* He banged his head on the inside of the canoe.

"Ouch," Patrick said. He rubbed his head as he crawled out of the canoe.

He looked up. Not a cloud was in sight. Birds called to each other from the trees.

The sun shone on the calm water. Patrick saw only signs of the storm. Tree branches lay broken on the beach. The sand was covered with the marks left by thousands of water droplets.

Patrick heard the sound of beating drums in the distance.

"Have those drums been beating all night?" Patrick asked.

"I don't know," Nettleton said. "I wouldn't have heard it. The rain be beatin' on top of me canoe."

Patrick's stomach growled. He couldn't remember the last time he'd eaten.

"Is there any food?" he asked.

"Food may be in the canoes' baskets," Nettleton said. "Help me unpack 'em."

The ropes that held down the baskets

were woven from plant leaves.

Patrick got out his pocketknife to cut the ropes. But Nettleton just pulled a loop, and the ropes fell free.

This thing is useless, Patrick thought. He put the knife back in his pocket.

Nettleton and Patrick looked through the baskets.

Inside one was a drum made out of a log.

"This must be like the ones that we heard beating," Patrick said. He took it out of the canoe. He set it on the ground.

"But ye can't eat it," Nettleton said. "What else be in there?"

One basket held yams and coconuts. Another basket was filled with short, fat bananas.

Patrick grabbed one and peeled back the yellow skin. He took a bite. It was sweeter than the ones he ate at home.

Nettleton opened the last basket. It contained reddish brown discs.

Patrick asked with his mouth full, "Are those turtle shells?"

"Aye, mate," Nettleton said. He grabbed a banana and pointed at the basket. "Those be from the backs of sea turtles. They be part of the cannibals' religion. Very valuable, I must say."

"And they belong to me," a deep voice said from behind them.

Patrick and Nettleton spun around.

A dark-skinned man with wild, tall, and frizzy hair stood near the canoe. His chest was bare except for a whale-tooth necklace.

"What be yer name?" Nettleton asked.

"I am Toki," the man said. "King of the cannibals."

Nettleton reared back and shook the banana at Toki. "Ye stay away from us," the surgeon's mate said. "In the name of Her Majesty—"

"Queen Victoria," Toki said. "I know about the queen. I will not harm the queen's officers."

Nettleton looked relieved.

Then Toki looked at Patrick with narrowed eyes. He said, "However, I claim this boy as my prisoner."

The Turtle Shell

"Your prisoner!" Patrick cried. "You . . . you can't. I'm already Captain Home's prisoner. And he'll be angry if you take me."

" 'Tis true," Nettleton said with a nod. "Captain Home be the boy's master."

Toki smiled. His white teeth glistened. He said, "I know about the Naval law. Captain Home must put fugitives on shore. The boy is now on *my* island. So he is *my* prisoner."

With a loud cry of "*Yi! Yi! Yi!*" Toki leaped

toward Patrick.

Patrick dove to one side.

The cannibal chief stumbled and rolled in the sand. He quickly got to his feet again.

Nettleton stepped between Toki and Patrick. "He be not yours!" Nettleton shouted.

Toki growled and pushed Nettleton aside. He spun to face Patrick. The king's arms were open wide like a bear ready to attack its prey.

Patrick didn't know what to do. Should he run into the forest or look for a weapon? He didn't dare leave Nettleton. What could he use—*his knife? A rock?* His eye fell on a turtle shell. It was about three feet wide. He remembered what Nettleton had said about the shells.

Patrick grabbed the shell. "Stop," Patrick

shouted at Toki, "or I'll break the shell!"

Patrick lifted the shell high. He acted as if he would smash it against a rock.

Toki stopped. He lowered his arms and cried, "You must not!"

"Go on, Patrick," Nettleton said as he got to his feet. "The shells be sacred. They be a sign of a cannibal king's power. Break it, and ye break Toki."

"You cannibals are crazy," Patrick said but kept the turtle shell held high. "You worry about a turtle shell. But you would joyfully make me your next meal. That's backward. You're supposed to protect *people*!"

Toki's face twisted up in anger. "You speak like the man Calvert! I hate his words! I hate the teachings of his God! Your God would be King and change our ways. He would make us weak with words like 'love your enemies.' I am *king*. I kill and eat my enemies."

"You can't be much of a king if you need a turtle shell for power," Patrick said.

Toki raised his fists and shook them. "I say fear Toki, king of the cannibals!" he shouted.

Patrick was afraid. He glanced at Nettleton. Nettleton's face had turned pale. But he seemed to gather courage. Nettleton stepped forward and asked, "If ye be a king, then where be yer tribesmen?" Toki glared at him.

"They died in the storm, didn't they?" Nettleton asked. "Yer heart be full of anger now."

Toki took a huge breath. He looked as if he might scream with rage again. Then the air went out of him. He shrank like an old balloon.

The change was so surprising that Patrick almost felt sorry for him. Toki looked helpless.

"Your Christian God took my best warriors in the storm," Toki said. "Calvert warned me. They are dead. I will be next."

"Ye don't have to be," Nettleton said. "Give up yer cannibal ways and ye might live."

"The Christian God will forgive you, if you let Him," Patrick added.

Toki looked at Patrick. The look of fear had been replaced by something else.

Toki stood up straight as if he had made a decision. "Bring me the drum," Toki said. "I will send a message."

Drumbeats

In the morning, Beth, Calvert, the soldiers, and the others left the cave. They returned to the rescue boat. Calvert's plan was to row around the shore to look for any sign of Patrick and Nettleton.

As they began to climb into the boat, Calvert stopped. He held up a hand and asked for silence. Everyone listened.

Beth heard the pounding of distant drums.

Calvert smiled. "The drums say that two white people have been found. They are on the eastern shore."

"Can we believe the drums?" Sergeant Dunn asked.

"I've never known them to lie," Calvert said.

"We'll row east, then," Sergeant Dunn said.

They climbed into the rescue boat and set off. It was a tight fit with the Fijian men aboard too.

Beth tipped her face toward the morning sky. The warmth made her feel at peace. But the feeling ended as soon as the drums began to beat again.

"What are the drums saying now?" Beth asked. She was afraid Patrick had been hurt. Or something worse.

The Fijians shuffled about nervously. They muttered to each other in their own language.

"What's wrong?" Beth asked.

Calvert put a hand on her shoulder. "Toki wants the Christians to come to get Patrick and Nettleton."

"But that's good news, right?" Beth asked. "Why is everyone so nervous?"

"The Fijians think he's using Patrick and Nettleton to lure us. It could be a trap," Calvert said.

"Would Toki do that?" Beth asked.

"I have known Toki for a long time," Calvert said. "He has broken every treaty he ever made. He has killed hundreds of Christians."

Beth frowned. "Why would Toki do such

terrible things?" she asked.

Calvert looked thoughtful. Then he said, "Toki rejects God, and so he rejects God's ways. He has no regard for human life. He doesn't understand virtues like honesty and respect."

Sergeant Dunn patted his rifle. He said, "If Toki thinks he can trap us without a fight, he's wrong. I hope he tries. I'd be happy to put a shot through him."

Beth looked at the other men in red coats. Their expressions were determined and grim.

"Please, let's not hope for bloodshed," Calvert said. "Our hope is to find Patrick and Nettleton and bring them to safety."

They rowed on. The rescue boat dipped and bobbed in the shallow waves. The water was choppy because the boat stayed close to the shoreline.

Beth focused her spyglass on the island. She searched for any sign of Patrick and Nettleton. Or even Toki.

She spied a white puff of smoke on the shore. She tugged at Calvert's sleeve. "Smoke," she said.

Calvert stood up in the boat and looked.

Beth asked, "Is it a camp? Are the cannibals burning more homes?"

Sergeant Dunn ordered the rowers to take the rescue boat closer the shore.

Beth looked through the spyglass again. She saw the source of all the smoke when they drew closer. There was a large fire. Through the smoke she thought she saw Nettleton. *And Patrick.*

"I see them!" Beth shouted. She jumped

up, rocking the boat.

"Are you certain?" Calvert asked.

She handed him her spyglass so he could look. "I'm sure it's them," she said.

Calvert frowned and handed the spyglass to Dunn.

Dunn peered through the lens a long time. "The smoke may be a trick. I think we should be prepared for an attack," Dunn said.

Dunn stood and spoke to the soldiers. "Rifles loaded," he said. "Prepare for battle."

Patrick watched as Nettleton stoked the signal fire. Nettleton threw some dried grass and wet branches on the growing flames. The smoke billowed up.

Patrick coughed.

Nettleton chuckled. "It will be easier for rescuers to spot the camp with a lot of smoke."

Patrick looked around for Toki. The cannibal had gone off to send the drum signal. But he hadn't come back. Patrick still didn't trust him.

Patrick looked out at the water. He blinked at something on the surface. Then he sprang to his feet. "It's the rescue boat!" he shouted.

Nettleton stood up and looked. He swung his arms back and forth

to clear away the
smoke.

"I knew they'd find us!"
Nettleton cried. Then he shouted,
"Over here!"

Patrick was about to run toward the
water. But Toki suddenly came up behind
them. He was holding a spear.

Nettleton turned to him. "What ye be doin'
with that spear?" he asked.

"Your men have rifles," Toki said. He put
a hand on Patrick's shoulder. Toki guided
Patrick toward the water. "They must see
that you are both safe. Move!"

Nettleton stood and walked away from

the fire. "Who be on board?" he asked. He moved toward the water. He stumbled into Patrick.

Nettleton's peg leg got caught in the sand. Patrick grabbed Nettleton's arm, trying to steady him. But both of them fell in a heap.

Toki was left standing on the beach holding a spear.

"There's too much smoke," Sergeant Dunn said. He still held Beth's spyglass. "Toki has a spear, but I can't see what he's doing."

Beth was worried. She leaned over the boat's side to see better.

"Wait," Dunn said. "Toki is forcing Patrick into the water. I think he's taken Patrick as a hostage!"

Thud!

The boat hit something in the water.

The jolt sent Beth tumbling overboard. The men in the boat shouted.

Beth went under the water. When she came up, a wave carried her farther out. The men in the boat stretched out their arms. But they couldn't reach her.

Another wave came, and it took her even farther from the boat. Beth swam toward the shore. But the waves tossed her one way and another. Her wet clothes dragged her down.

She heard shouts from the rescue boat. Dunn shouted, "Toki knocked Nettleton down! He's got a spear!"

Then she heard Calvert shout, "Hold your fire! Watch out for the girl! Steer the boat around!"

Dunn shouted something about the coral reef. Then Beth went under again.

Patrick and Nettleton untangled themselves. Patrick pushed himself up with his arm.

He saw Beth flapping her arms in the water.

Is she drowning? he wondered. Patrick climbed to his feet.

"Beth!" Patrick shouted. "I'm coming to help you!"

Patrick sprinted toward the water.

Suddenly, Toki pushed him roughly aside.

Patrick fell onto his knees. "Hey!" he shouted. He struggled to get up again.

Toki rushed forward. He lifted his spear and then gave a loud cry. Toki threw the spear at Beth with all his might.

"Stop!" Patrick cried.

Then a shot rang out. *Bang!*

Toki's body jerked. He fell backward into the surf.

Patrick saw blood drip from Toki's shoulder. The dark blood spread into the water. A wave pushed the fallen king onto the sand.

Nettleton rushed forward. He waved his arms at the rescue boat. "Don't shoot!" he called out. "Toki be down!"

Patrick looked for Beth. She was still flapping her arms in the water. Toki's spear must have missed her.

So where did it go? he wondered. *Why did Toki throw it?*

The rescue boat was nearer. On board, Calvert was shouting something to a soldier.

A group of Fijians shouted, "*Bole! Bole!*" They picked up their spears and leaped into the water.

What in the world is going on? Patrick wondered.

Patrick looked all around. He saw Beth pull herself out of the water farther up the beach. She had something in her hand.

Next Patrick watched Nettleton. The surgeon's mate leaned over Toki. He looked as if he were whispering to the cannibal king. But Patrick couldn't hear the words.

Then Patrick looked to the water. The rescue boat came closer. The Fijians splashed toward him.

"Are you here to save us or kill us?" Patrick called out. But no one was listening.

Toki's Last Battle

Beth bobbed in the water. She was staring at Toki's spear and a dead stingray. Toki's spear had sliced through its blue-and-yellow body. She hadn't realized the stingray had been nearby. She must have stepped on it and made it angry.

Beth tried to stay afloat, but it wasn't easy. She had to flap one arm a lot.

When the waves lulled, she looked at the shore. Patrick seemed to be frantic.

Toki was lying on the sand with Nettleton near him.

And then a wave drove her onto another part of the beach.

Toki saved my life, she thought.

Patrick stood where he was, watching her. "Are you all right?" he shouted.

"Yes!" she called back. She left the spear and the dead stingray. "I'm coming!"

Patrick waved to her. Then he jogged over to the crowd of Fijians circling the fallen Toki.

Dripping wet, Beth also ran over. She squeezed in next to Patrick.

Patrick and Beth gave each other a quick nod. Patrick seemed worried.

Beth turned to Toki who was lying face up on the sand. She put a hand to her mouth.

Toki's eyes were closed. His body lay still. Blood poured from a wound near his shoulder.

Nettleton knelt near Toki's body. "I need a knife!" he said.

One of the Fijians offered him a long blade.

Nettleton shook his head. "Too big," he said. "I be needin' a small knife to get this bullet out. Someone must have one."

Beth suddenly remembered Patrick's pocketknife. She turned to him.

Patrick seemed to remember it at the same time. He pulled out the pocketknife. "Will this do?" he asked. He handed it to the surgeon's mate.

"It be perfect," he said. He opened the

blade. He then took it over to the fire. He put the knife in the flames.

Nettleton is burning germs off the knife, Beth thought.

"Will he be all right?" Beth asked.

"I don't know," Nettleton replied.

"Pray that Nettleton can help him," Patrick said softly.

Nettleton came back. He began poking the small knife into Toki's shoulder.

Beth winced and then looked away.

Just then, Calvert and Dunn joined the circle.

"Are you well?" Calvert asked Beth.

"He probably saved my life," she said and nodded toward Toki. "He killed a stingray with his spear."

Calvert looked at Dunn.

Dunn frowned. "I thought he was trying to kill the girl," he said. "I didn't want to risk her life."

Toki groaned. All eyes returned to him. Nettleton stuck the knife inside Toki's shoulder again. This time, the knife lifted out a bullet.

Beth was surprised by the bullet's size. It was as large as a shooter marble.

More blood flowed from Toki's shoulder. Beth had to look away.

"I need some healin' leaves," Nettleton said. He looked to the Fijians. "It grows on the ground. Do ye know which plant that be?"

"*Wa bosucu,*" a Fijian said. He ran off.

Another Fijian spoke to Calvert in his language. Calvert replied. Then he saw Beth watching them.

"He wants to know what will happen if Toki lives," Calvert said. "They are afraid that Toki will want revenge for his wound."

"Will he?" Beth asked.

Calvert nodded and said, "That is why we must now pray for the evil in his soul. We must ask God to remove it, like Nettleton removed that bullet."

Suddenly Toki's eyes fluttered open. He gasped loudly. Everyone tensed.

Toki reached a hand toward Calvert. "Tell your God to spare me," he said in a small voice.

Calvert clasped Toki's hand. "I will, Toki," he said. Then Calvert lifted his hands.

"Dear God," Calvert prayed aloud, "we pray for this wounded man. Heal his body, his mind, and his soul. Bring his heart to

repent and to know Your peace. Amen."

"If your God allows me to live," Toki said in a harsh whisper, "I promise I will no longer kill Christians."

Calvert and Toki stared at one another.

"Do you repent?" Calvert asked.

"I repent," Toki said. He looked at the Fijian men. "Forgive me for all I have done to your village and your people. Please . . . forgive me."

Then Toki closed his eyes again

Good-byes

Nettleton pressed the healing leaves against Toki's wound. "This will help his pain," Nettleton said. "He be needin' to board the ship. His wound needs stichin' up."

The soldiers lifted Toki and carried him to a ramp. It lead from the shore to the boat. *A sailor must have put it there when the boat landed*, she thought.

Nettleton came to Patrick and Beth. "I can't stay," he said. "I must return to the ship. Ye will have to fend for yerselves for now."

"That's a funny thing to tell a prisoner," Patrick said.

Nettleton smiled. "Not a prisoner," he said. He reached out his hand. "A *friend* ye be to me."

Patrick shook his hand.

"This be yers," Nettleton said. He held the knife out to Patrick. "It be much appreciated."

Patrick pushed his hand away. "The knife is yours to keep," he said. "You'll need it when you are promoted to ship's surgeon."

"Thank ye kindly," Nettleton said. He then gave a slight salute to Beth. "All the best to ye, miss."

Nettleton limped off to the boat ramp.

Calvert had been talking to the group of Fijians. He now walked over to Patrick and Beth. The three of them watched people board the rescue boat.

"Will Captain Home allow Toki on the ship?" Beth asked Calvert. "He said he'd never allow a cannibal on board."

"I believe Toki is no longer a cannibal," Calvert said. "Captain Home would not refuse to help him now."

Dunn called to the missionary, "Mr. Calvert, you should return with us. You'll have to explain everything to the captain."

Calvert held up his hand. "I think you're right," he said. He turned to Beth and Patrick. "The Christian Fijians will watch over you until I return to help bring peace."

Before Beth could say anything, she

heard a familiar humming sound. She looked toward the forest. At the edge sat the Imagination Station.

She nudged Patrick. He had seen it too.

"We're in good hands," Beth said. She gave Calvert a hug. "Thank you for everything."

Calvert gave her a fond look. It was a final good-bye, and he seemed to know it. He put his hand on her shoulder and squeezed it gently.

"You'll do great things if you let our great God work through you," Calvert said. "Never be afraid to go where He leads."

"Yes, sir," she said.

Calvert shook Patrick's hand. "Take care of her," he said. He turned and hurried to the boat ramp.

The Fijians had wandered to the burned

huts. Beth thought they were looking for valuables that escaped the fire.

Now that the cousins had privacy, Beth smiled at Patrick. "I leave you alone and you nearly get eaten by a shark . . . and a cannibal," she said.

A smile crossed his lips. "It's a good thing you came to rescue me," he said.

"Don't you forget it," she said. She suddenly hugged him.

Patrick blushed and endured the hug for a few seconds. Then he stepped away.

Patrick glanced at the Imagination Station. He said, "I'm ready. Let's go."

Beth nodded.

They climbed into the Imagination Station. The door slid closed.

Patrick pushed the red button.

The Workshop

The door to the Imagination Station slid open. Beth climbed out of the machine first. Patrick followed.

Whit was sitting at his workbench. "So you decided to have an Imagination Station adventure," he said, arms folded.

"Yes!" Patrick said. His voice was full of excitement. "We got to meet a man with a peg leg and a cannibal and—"

Beth nudged Patrick hard. "I don't think

that's what he meant," she said.

Patrick looked unsure. Then he seemed to remember. "Oh. Uh. That's right," he said. "We should have asked permission first. I'm sorry."

Whit stood and walked to the Imagination Station. He tipped his head and seemed to relax. "Just so it doesn't happen again," he said. "I'd hate to have to put a lock on the machine." He patted the side of the Imagination Station.

"It won't happen again," Patrick said.

"I'm sorry, too," Beth added.

Whit gave them a reassuring smile. "So you met the missionary James Calvert," he said. "What did you think of him?"

"He was amazing," Beth said. "I've never known anyone like him—except maybe you."

Whit chuckled. He said, "Not many people cared about telling the cannibal tribes about Jesus. But Calvert and other missionaries gave their lives to do it. There were tens of thousands of Fijian Christians when Calvert left Fiji. And the cannibalism had stopped."

"That's what was so great," Beth said. "Toki had done a lot of evil things. But Mr.

Calvert kept reaching out to him."

"That's what Jesus calls us to do," Whit said. "We're supposed to pray for our enemies and give freely to others. Even people we don't like."

Patrick hung his head. He said, "Oh. I get it now."

"Get what?" Whit asked.

"I was in a really bad mood when I came to Whit's End," Patrick said.

"I was feeling sorry for myself. I didn't want to give up my soccer game for grandma's party. I was even mean to Beth. But she didn't hold a grudge. She came to save me on the island."

"That sounds like a good summary," Whit said gently.

Patrick gave Beth an embarrassed look. "I'm sorry," he said.

Whit said, "I'm proud of both of you."

The cousins looked at him, surprised.

"You both acted bravely even though you didn't have to," Whit said.

Beth smiled. Patrick looked down and shuffled his feet.

Whit rubbed his hands together after a few seconds of silence. "I believe the line of customers is gone upstairs. How about some ice cream?" he asked.

"I'd love some," Beth said.

"Me, too," Patrick said.

"Good," Whit said. He turned and walked up the stairs to the main floor.

Patrick and Beth stayed in the workshop.

"Beth," he said, "I would enjoy it a lot more if you went to Grandma's party with me."

"Of course I'll go," Beth said. "Last time we were apart, you got into trouble."

The two of them laughed together. Then they went up the stairs for ice cream.

Secret Word Puzzle

Fill in the eight clues. Then you'll know the secret word and the name of Captain Home's ship.

1 The cannibals ride in these wood boats:

⬜ ___ ___ ___ ___ ___ (page 14)

2 Patrick is scared of this sea creature:

___ ___ ⬜ ___ ___ (page 64)

3 The missionary's last name:

___ ___ ⬜ ___ ___ ___ ___ (page 26)

4 White canvas hanging on a ship's mast:

___ ___ ___ ⬜ (page 9)

5 The name of the cannibals' islands:

___ ⬜ ___ ___ (page 45)

6 Another name for a South Pacific storm:

___ ___ ___ ___ [ ] ___ ___ (page 47)

7 Beth used this to look at the island:

___ [ ] ___ ___ ___ ___ ___ (page 14)

8 Things that can open a lock:

___ [ ] ___ ___ (page 39)

Each answer has a letter in a box. Write those letters, in order, in the boxes below. The answer is the secret word:

1 [ ] 2 [ ] 3 [ ] 4 [ ] 5 [ ] 6 [ ] 7 [ ] 8 [ ]

Questions about Battle for Cannibal Island

Q: Did the Fijian cannibals really eat people?

A: *Sadly, yes. Cannibals killed their enemies and others for religious sacrifice. The missionaries helped stop this terrible practice by teaching the Fijians Bible lessons.*

Q: Did James Calvert have a family?

A: *Yes, a big one! He married a woman named Mary, and they had several children. When each child turned about eight years old, he or she was sent to England to go to school.*

For more info on James Calvert and Fiji, visit **TheImaginationStation.com**.

AUTHOR WAYNE THOMAS BATSON divides his time between family, teaching, and writing. He also likes to read, golf, play video games, travel to the beach, play electric guitar, and create 3D artwork.

AUTHOR MARIANNE HERING is the former editor of *Focus on the Family Clubhouse®* magazine. She has written more than a dozen children's books. She likes to read out loud in bed to her fluffy gray-and-white cat, Koshka.

ILLUSTRATOR DAVID HOHN draws and paints books, posters, and projects of all kinds. He works from his studio in Portland, Oregon.

Start an adventure!
with Focus on the Family

Whether you're looking for new ways to teach young children about God's Word, entertain active imaginations with exciting adventures or help teenagers understand and defend their faith, we can help. For trusted resources to help your kids thrive, visit our online Family Store at:

FOCUS ON THE FAMILY®

No matter who you are, what you're going through, or what challenges your family may be facing, we're here to help. With practical resources —like our toll-free Family Help Line, counseling, and Web sites— we're committed to providing trustworthy, biblical guidance, and support.

Focus on the Family Clubhouse Jr.

Creative stories, fascinating articles, puzzles, craft ideas, and more are packed into each issue of *Focus on the Family Clubhouse Jr.*® magazine. You'll love the way this bright and colorful magazine reinforces biblical values and helps boys and girls (ages 3–7) explore their world. **Subscribe now at Clubhousejr.com.**

Focus on the Family Clubhouse

Through an appealing combination of encouraging content and entertaining activities, *Focus on the Family Clubhouse*® magazine (ages 8–12) will help your children—or kids you care about—develop a strong Christian foundation. **Subscribe now at Clubhousemagazine.com.**

Go to FocusOnTheFamily.com or call us at 800-A-FAMILY (232-6459)

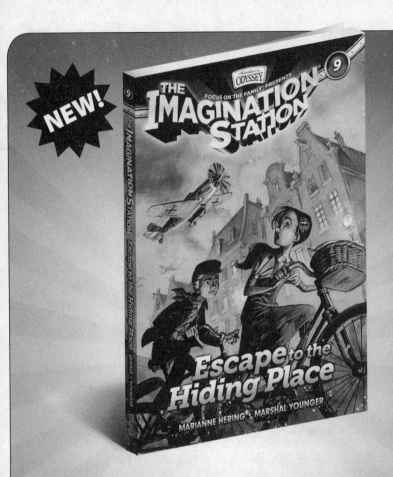

World War Two has come to Holland

. . . and so have Patrick and Beth. The Dutch Resistance workers give the cousins a secret mission: smuggling a Jewish baby to her mother. Time is running out. Patrick and Beth must race to the hiding place to save the baby's future. But the Germans are everywhere: the woods, the roads, the city, and even the sky. Is there really a hiding place? Or will the Germans find that, too?